Wrong Channel

Those Crazy Tanner Kids

Mike Jackson

ISBN-13:
978-1492340294

ISBN-10:
1492340294

DEDICATION

With love to my wife Natasha and my kids Olivia,
Seth, Paul, Benson and Daniel

CONTENTS

.

The Castle

Saturday, the next to last in October, when the air was warm enough not to wear a coat but not so hot so as to be uncomfortable, seven year-old Grace turned from the knot hole in the fence to her younger brothers.

"I think we should ask to play in Jasmine's castle."

Bobby, Stephen and Jason, did not reply, but crisscrossed the lawn, as they chased the robin from the deck railing to the fence and back again.

"Come on guys, we almost got it that time," said five year-old Bobby, the oldest of the three.

Cheeks flushed, blue-eyed almost four year-old Stephen huffed, "Maybe we should throw something at it to slow it down."

"Burd," said toddler Jason as he charged the bird, triggering a sprint by his older brothers.

"Guys," called Grace from her position at the fence.

"We're doing some work! We'll help you when we're not busy trying to get this guy," shouted Bobby as he overtook Jason.

"We'll have a lot of fun," responded Grace in a singsong voice.

Trailing his older brother slightly, Stephen sang, "No, we won't. Mrs. Vandeslushy don't like us."

"That's because Bobby put junk on her doorstep. It's Bobby's fault," said Grace.

Bobby stopped mid-step. "No, I didn't put junk there. I made her a treat."

"A treat that tastes like poo poo," said Grace.

Stephen covered his mouth. "That's potty talk, Grace."

Grace stepped towards her brothers. "Come on you guys. Come ask to play with me. You don't have to come in the yard. Just come ask with me."

Bobby and Stephen looked to each other and then to Grace. "No."

"Fine." Grace grabbed a plastic golf club and held it over her shoulder. "You can't have any fun then."

The boys stood with mouths hanging open as the club left their sister's hand and flew directly at the bird. It struck the fence near enough to the bird that the offended robin bolted from the yard.

"I'm telling Mom on you," said Bobby. "We're not 'posed to throw stuff at the birds. Mom said so."

"You guys acknored me," said Grace.

"No we didn't," cried Stephen.

"I'm telling on you that you tried to smack our bird buddy," said Bobby.

"Then I'll tell Mom you stole a fruit snack," threatened Grace.

"Well, I'll... I'll tell Mom you threw something at a bird," said Bobby.

"You're gonna get in more trouble cause I'll tell two things to Mom."

"You're mean," responded Bobby.

"That's three things. Acknoring, stealing, and calling names." Grace held up a finger with each offense. "You're in trouble."

"If you go tell then your gonna have to go inside and we'll tell Mom on you for being mean and using potty-talk," said Stephen.

"No I didn't," said Grace.

"Yes, you did. You said poo poo," said Stephen.

Grace now covered her mouth. "You said potty talk. You're in as much trouble as Bobby."

"I was just saying what you said. You're not my best friend any more, Grace," replied Stephen.

"Fine, I don't need you guys. I'm going to play lots of fun games with Jasmine in the castle and I'm going to tell her never to let you play with her again. I'll go and play in the castle everyday and laugh at you from the tower."

"You're not gonna be allowed to play 'cause you're a bad girl," said Bobby.

"Yes, I will."

"You're too chicken to go without us," said Stephen.

"No, I'm not." Grace pivoted from the boys and stomped away. It wasn't long before she was around the corner of the house and out of sight.

Marie and Jim, the parents of Grace, Bobby, Stephen and Jason, the Tanner kids, lounged next to each other on the hand-me down floral patterned couch in the living room of the home. Alone time, whether they liked it or not, often became *collapse on the couch time* due to the shear exhaustion of late nights, the strain of the constant repetition of what should have been simple instructions and the never ending cleaning duties.

"One month, Jim," said Marie sleepily, her head rested against her husband's arm.

"Hmm?" Jim asked.

"One month since my belly started to show," said Marie.

"Oh. That's good. Only a few more to go." Using the remote control, Jim turned the volume on the television up one notch

"Come on. Play the game with me. I'll go again." Marie nestled in closer to her husband. She grabbed the remote and muted the sound altogether. "Three days."

Jim straightened up. "Three days since I've had to fetch Grace's boot off the roof because the boys chucked it up there?"

"No."

"Three days since the boys thought it would be a good idea if they all went to the bathroom all day in the same toilet without aiming or flushing?"

"No."

"Three days since Grace informed me I was using the word *approval* incorrectly?"

"No. You are not even close."

"A little hint then?"

"Okay. It's about me."

"Three days since you last had a shower?"

"Jim!" Marie sat straight up.

"I was joking. Bad joke. Bad joke." Jim tried to snuggle in.

Marie shifted from him. "So you think I smell bad?"

"No, I didn't mean it that way, I was just, it was, I wasn't thinking. I was just trying to be funny."

"I didn't think it was funny."

"I'm sorry." Jim hesitantly leaned in again, watching for what her reaction to his movement would be.

"What I meant was it's been three days since I had morning sickness."

"That's great," he said with a kiss on her forehead. "I sure hope it keeps up."

"I guess you would. Throw up would only make me more stinky."

"I'm so sorry. I take it back. Rewinding. Deleting. Please, forgive me.

"Fine. It's your turn," said Marie.

"Okay. My turn. Twelve minutes."

"Hmm. Are you talking about the length of time it takes for something to happen or the length of time since something happened?"

"You have to guess."

"You have to at least give me a clue. Besides, I didn't make you guess. Why do I have to guess?"

"Because it's my riddle and I want you to guess. It'll be fun."

"I don't have to guess. I'm not that anxious to know," she said with arms crossed.

"Okay, okay. It has been twelve minutes since we last spoke to the kids about behaving themselves or showing restraint or anything like it."

Marie smiled and after a pause said, "Why did you have to go and jinx it by saying something about it?"

The Siege

Three classes of apples

Unripe Apples: *generally off limits - not good for throwing - small and no splat -not good for eating - too sour.*

Ready to Eat Apples*: good for eating - very sweet - only so-so for throwing - no splat.*

Rotten Apples*: not good for eating - mushy, gross and stinky - perfect for throwing - splat.*

Through the fence boards, Stephen saw his big sister being led across the yard. "Look," he gasped. "Jasmine is taking Grace prisoner in the castle. We've got to help her!"

Without further instruction, Jason began throwing air punches, accenting each attack with an appropriate sound effect, imaginary villains falling helplessly by the wayside.

Bobby edged Stephen over and looked through the same gap. Having looked, he backed away slowly. "No, you guys," he said solemnly as he turned towards his younger brothers. "Grace is the enemy. Just like I told you. Look, she's playing with Jasmine Vandyslushe. She's gonna play in the castle without us."

"Grace is a meanie," Stephen whispered.

"It's time to teach Grace not to not let us get to play in the castle," Bobby growled as he eyed the unripe apple Jason had stuffed in the front pocket of his overalls. Ignoring Jason's protests, Bobby took the apple, turned to his brothers and explained, "Let's get her."

On the neighbor's side of the fence, glad she had been brave enough to invite herself to play with

12

Jasmine, Grace stood in the tower of the castle. She wore Jasmine's best pretend-princess dress. She looked over the clusters of dandelions that adorned the vast green domain that spread before her. "Truly, my kingdom is the finest and the most beautiful of all kingdoms. Servant? Bring me a snack."

"Yes, your majesty," was the reply from the bowels of the castle.

"As we discussed, servant, you are not to tell the evil queens about my calling you servant or making you bring me snacks. They wouldn't understand."

"Evil queens?" asked Jasmine.

Grace slipped out of character and whispered. "Our moms, remember?"

"Right. Why not, my lady?"

"Because my mom," Grace paused and resumed her royal demeanor. "I mean the evil queen, doesn't like it when I boss... I mean when I am a princess because of my great beauty. And your mom, well, she doesn't need to know either."

Jasmine rested her elbow on the wall and her head in her hand. She sighed. "I don't know how you bear it. I mean being so beautiful."

"I know." Grace flipped her hair. "It is a difficult burden to bear. Enough chitchat. Where is my cake?"

Within moments, Jasmine arose out of the depths of the castle with the lid of an ice cream bucket covered in mud, rocks, grass and dandelion seed. "My lady, your cake."

"You have a gift, servant. That will do. You may return to your quar—" Cut off mid-sentence by a thud, Grace searched for the source of the sound.

"Ouch." Jasmine was pelted in the back of the head. "Your majesty, what was that?"

A high-pitched war cry sounded in the distance, immediately followed a hailstorm of projectiles. At first, most of the objects fell short of the castle, landing harmlessly on the grass.

"You guys stop it right..." A rotten apple burst as it struck the edge of the tower, spraying rotten apple flesh all over the girls' beautiful dresses. Apples continued to fly, now more accurate than before.

On the other side of the fence and after a flurry of activity, Bobby held up his hand to lift the assault. All had gone quiet in the castle. They were out of rotten apples and had had to resort to the ripe ones. Their attack had been helter-skelter until they heard the girls scream. With that success, Stephen had stopped throwing indiscriminately and had become a marksman, taking aim, launching his apple at the target and yelling each time he heard a scream on the other side. Jason's apples did not actually go over the fence but the wrap of the apples against the wooden boards heightened the intensity of the attack. He had been the first one to catapult.

Ding-dong

Marie and Jim simultaneously raised their right fists to face each other and counted, bobbing their fists with each number, "One, Two, Three." At the end of the countdown, Marie kept her hand balled up while Jim held his index finger and middle finger up in the shape of peace sign.

"That's all you." Marie motioned towards the door. "Go on. It was fair."

"Best two out of three?" Jim asked.

Marie shook her head. "Rock beats scissors. Those are the rules of the game. I'm going to go check on the kids. They've been quiet for too long." Marie walked out of the living room into the kitchen.

Jim opened the door just as the doorbell was pressed for the second time. "Oh. Hi, Mrs. Vandersluis. How are you today?"

Standing with Grace in one hand and her daughter in the other, she, resembling an eggplant more than a person, face swollen and eyes set. "Not well," Mrs. Vandersluis began, her voice trembling with rage, "I am here to talk to you about your children."

"Oh boy..." said Jim.

"Out of the kindness of my heart I allowed your daughter to play with Jasmine —against my better judgment," Mrs. Vandersluis began, "I allowed Grace to play at my house because I am such a good neighbor," she paused for effect, "and now she has been the cause of this," she concluded, hissing as she motioned to the satiny dresses splattered with apple remnants.

Jim reached out to the dresses. "I'm so sorry. Leave the dresses with me and..."

"You're sorry, are you? My Jasmine and your" another dramatic pause punctuated with a somber shake of her head "daughter were each wearing one of these when your boys... Look at this, there are ruined. "

Jim took the dresses. "If we can't clean them, we'll replace them."

Meanwhile, the boys had come in from the backyard and caught sight of what was happening at the front door. Bobby immediately retreated back outside, followed by his shadow, Jason. The sight of Grace and Jasmine with apple chunks in their hair seized hold on poor Stephen. He was yanked towards them as if by a space-age tractor beam. The closer he got, the louder his laugh became.

"Stephen!" Jim snapped through clenched teeth.

Tears welled up in the big eyes that had so recently been full of fun. He turned and walked up the stairs, his quiet sobbing drifting down.

"What a villain!" Mrs. Vandersluis hiked her pants up with the tips of her fingers. "Some children have no hope. Your wife seems like a decent enough person. It seems that wasn't enough to overcome the... the... defects. Perhaps your youngest will mercifully beat the odds."

"That was all very interesting." Jim grabbed Grace and pulled her in the house when the woman momentarily released her grip to tug her pants over her belly flap. "Thanks for the visit. Sorry about your dresses, Jasmine. We will either get them cleaned or we'll replace them." The neighbor opened her mouth but Jim interrupted with "Goodbye." He closed the door — and locked it.

"Grace, I do not want you to do what Daddy just did, okay?"

Grace looked at the door then back at her dad. "You don't want me to slam the door in the neighbor's face?"

Jim's shoulders slumped slightly. "I didn't slam the..."

Marie opened the kitchen door and walked towards the front door. "Did you slam the door on Carol?"

"No, I only closed the door quickly. I thought the conversation was over."

"But her mouth was opened, Daddy."

Marie finished looking out the curtained windows on the side of the door, apparently satisfied that Carol Vandersluis was no longer there. "Daddy was actually helping our neighbor. If you can't say something nice, you shouldn't say it. By closing the door, Daddy made it so Mrs. Vandersluis couldn't break that rule."

Jim mouthed a "thank you" to Marie. He headed up the stairs. Hearing young voices, he stopped just outside of Bobby and Stephen's room.

"Daddy's mad at me for being a bad boy." There was a tormented moan, then he continued, "He's never going to like me again."

An older voice cut in. "Dad just losed his madness for a bit. He's just mad 'cause we threw away all the mushy apples so now he can't eat apple sauce every all the day long."

Another wail from the younger boy. "Now he's mad at me for twenty-hundred things. For coming to say 'hi' to Mrs. Vandeslushy, for throwing all the mushy apples away and for being mean to Grace."

"We wasn't being mean to Grace. We was trying to save her from the Vandeslushy's. Right, Jason?" asked the older boy.

The youngest boy responded with a hearty, "Yep."

"See. Once Daddy's temperature gots down to cooler than right now, he won't be mad at us anymore. 'member when I peed in Grace's boot?" asked Bobby.

There was a choking sound followed by a loud guffaw. "Uh huh. That was so funny."

"It sure was," Bobby said through maniacal laughter.

"Yep," said Jason.

Jim poked his head around the corner. Stephen sat on the bottom bunk bed. Bobby, to his right, had his arm wrapped around him. Jason standing on the floor and to his left patted Stephen's leg. All three were laughing, even Stephen, his face tear-stained.

They went silent as Jim stepped fully into view. "I need you boys to come outside with me. If we don't pick up all those apples, how am I going to be able to eat apple sauce every day all the day long?"

Stephen looked in awe at his older brother. Jason laughed.

"But before we go outside, will you please apologize to your sister?" Jim asked.

"Ycs, Dad," the bunch cried as they scurried out of the room, from oldest to youngest, to apologize to their sister and undo some of the carnage they'd unleashed that day.

A Mighty Leap

Precariously perched, Bobby overlooked his surroundings. The forces of evil would have little chance against his great agility and strength. He crouched like a frog ready to hop. "Feel my justice!" The powerful contraction of his quadriceps propelled him off the now spinning computer chair and into the air. And then gravity took over.

Whack.

"Mom!" The chair still spinning, his teeth covered in blood, the cast still on his arm from his last daring adventure, a bawling Bobby bolted to the kitchen.

"What happened?" exclaimed Marie, as she scooped Bobby up. "Are you okay?" She carried him to the kitchen sink.

"My face hurts. Is it gonna fall off?" he cried.

Marie sat him next to the sink. "No, you'll be fine. I just need to wash this so I can see what happened."

Bobby bum scooted away from the sink with his hands over his mouth.

Marie wet a towel. "Look. I'm going to use this very soft towel to clean your face so it will feel better. Okay?"

Bobby shook his head, his hands now plastered more firmly to his face.

"Come here," she said as she stepped closer and put a hand on his arm. "I'll be very gentle. You'll see. Just let me... see."

Having encouraged one hand away from his mouth, Bobby dropped the other but pursed his lips. Marie gently wiped the blood off of the face of the flinching boy. "Is that better?"

"A little," he whimpered.

Shifting him back to the sink, she tilted his head back. "Can you open your mouth please?"

"How come?" he asked, pressing his chin into his chest, making inspecting his mouth nearly impossible.

"Lift your chin, please. No, Bobby. Lift it up. No like this," she explained, placing her finger under his chin and forcing his head back. "I'm looking in your mouth so I can make sure you still have all of your teeth?"

"Okay." Bobby stared at the roof, his mouth gaped. Marie hovered in close to survey the damage. "Mom?"

"Yes," Marie answered, dabbing at his mouth and teeth with the wet cloth.

"Your breath kind of stinks."

"That's a rude thing to point out while I'm helping you."

"It's making me feel sick."

Marie turned her head. "Is this better?"

"Yeah. Lots better. Mom?"

"Are you going to tell me my breath stinks again?"

"No."

"Okay, then, what is it?"

"Will the tooth fairy give me money for the teeth that fell out?"

"She won't have to, you didn't lose any teeth. Can you spit into the sink, please."

With string hanging from his lip to the sink drain, he moaned. "No fair."

"Wouldn't you rather have teeth?" Marie swept the drool.

Bobby wiped his face with his sleeve. "I guess so."

"I guess so? What, do you want to look like you're eighty-seven years old? Do you want to have dentures when you're eight?"

"What are dentures?"

"Fake teeth."

"Can you get them like a vampire?"

"No."

"Oh. I guess I'm glad to have my teeth." Marie re-wet the cloth. She wiped the last of the blood from his face. A canyon-like wound on his lip was far beyond being fixed with a Band-Aid.

"Keep this cloth on your lip. You are going to have to get stitches."

"No fair."

"I'm sorry that seems no fair to you, but we've got to fix your lip or you're going to look like a man with two mouths, this one and another one sideways on your lip."

"Like an octopus. I don't want two lips 'cause then I'll have to live in the ocean and eat panomenans."

"Panomenans?"

"Uh huh. Grace said someday I'd get turned into an octopus 'cause I was bad and would have to eat panomenans. She said they taste like boogers. I don't want to eat boogers."

Marie did not remind him she had caught him earlier that morning sampling his own. "Calm down, I was just being silly about your mouth. You are not going to become an octopus so you can stop worrying about that. Do you believe me?"

"I guess so."

"I guess so?"

"Yah, I believe you, Mom. You're too pretty to tell lies."

"Thank you. Are you okay by yourself for a minute?"

"No."

"I've got to wake up Jason and get Stephen ready to go."

"Where are you going?"

"I'm going to take you to get fixed up."

"But I want Daddy to take me to get fixed up."

"Daddy's at work and he can't... Okay, we'll call your dad."

Stitches

Strings of blue vinyl seats rimmed with metal frames, peppered with people, some with bandaged heads, some in wheel chairs, others with grey faces, lined the large room where Bobby nestled under his father's arm. They were of all ages, genders and all classes, the rich and the poor, the old and the young. The automatic doors opened now and again cutting the sound of the fans circulating the air in the place.

Jim checked his watch. He had barely settled into work when he received the phone call. Mr. Jensen, his boss, was not sympathetic. "Jim," he gruffly pronounced, "You've got no vacation days left. Your son will cost you a half-day's pay. If you're back at one minute after one, he'll cost you a full one."

Money was tight and would only be tighter if the emergency room trip extended beyond lunch. Bobby lifted the damp cloth from his mouth. "Daddy when are they gonna fix my lip up?"

"Pretty soon," he answered.

Pretty soon stretched into seconds, then minutes and finally into hours. A nurse entered the room, as she had many times before, and announced, "James Silverton, Horatio Burns and Robert Tanner."

Jim leapt to his feet with Bobby in his arms. He hurried to the nurse, put Bobby down and followed her from the mumble of the waiting room, through the swinging doors and into a long corridor lined with doors and gurneys. White tiles covered the floor, the walls were a pastel pink and water or some other liquid spotted the roof.

Bobby stopped and pointed at the wall. "What's that there? Hey, how come there's that space box on the wall?"

"That's a soap dispenser," Jim replied.

Bobby resisted. "Can it shoot like a cannon?"

"No, it is a soap dispenser." Jim successfully pulled Bobby forward.

"Hey lady, are they going to chop off my lip?" Bobby asked the pear shaped nurse as they made their way down an interminable hallway.

"No, we're just going to fix it up," she responded.

"This floor's squeaky," said Bobby as he shuffled down the hallway.

Jim put a finger to his lips "Shhh. There are sick people here and squeaking your shoes makes it worse for them."

"Why come?" asked Bobby.

"Because it hurts their ears," replied Jim.

33

"What if their ears got blowed off because they wented too fast down a slide?"

"I don't think anyone here lost their ears."

"Actually," the nurse interrupted, "there's a little boy who squeaked his shoes so much his ears jumped off his head and ran away forever."

"Oh," said Bobby as he covered his ears. His shuffle instantaneously transformed into a march.

After passing many doors, corridors and windows, the nurse stopped at an open door. "Here's your room guys, I'll be back with the doctor in a few minutes to get Robert ready."

"Thank you," Jim said.

"Thank you," Bobby mimicked as he smacked the woman on the backside.

Jim stuttered, "Bobby, what, what are you doing? I'm so sorry."

"I don't know," Bobby said.

Mouth gaped, the red from her rosy cheeks now spread to her entire face, the lady stood for enough time to be contemplating a harassment lawsuit. Fortunately her visage softened and she patted Bobby on the head. "You know it's not nice to touch someone like that."

"But Daddy does it to Mommy."

The woman shot a look at Jim, her small eyes challenging him, "no, it's not what you think. Just a playful tap."

Bobby smiled, "I think Mommy likes it."

Face unreadable, huffing, she turned on the spot and walked down the hallway. "Are you trying to get Daddy arrested?"

The room was not large, smaller than the average bedroom, fitted with a sink which was crowned with cupboards, a very mechanical looking bed and a computer system hooked up to an extendable arm on the wall. Having guided Bobby to the stool next to the computer, Jim stepped away and towards the mechanical bed. "Why did you do that?"

"Do what?" responded Bobby as he sat on the stool.

"Why did you hit that lady?"

"I don't know."

"Son, you can't touch someone else's private parts."

"But you touch Momma's bum bum." *Bum bum* was an okay word in the Tanner home, the duplication of the word softening its crude effect.

"But, um, well, Mommy and Daddy are married. When we were married we promised we'd only be with each other, and as a part of that Daddy is allowed to touch Mommy."

"So when you're married you can spank each other," asked Bobby.

"No. What I mean is, Bobby, some day you will meet a girl that you love very much..."

"Like Mommy?" Bobby asked.

"Yes, someone like Mommy."

"No, not someone *like* Mommy; it will *be* Mommy."

"No Bobby, Mommy is your mommy, so you can't marry your mommy."

Arms now crossed and head bowed, Bobby stated, "No fair."

"What do you mean it's not fair? You want to take Mommy away from me?"

"No."

"Did you know that right now there might be a little girl somewhere who's getting ready to get married to you?"

"Gross."

"You'll appreciate it more when you grow up." Jim looked out the window to the parking lot where cars lined up next to each other, row by row, each divided by a yellow line, the whole looking like a mosaic. Maybe he was thinking about his past, maybe Bobby's future, but whatever it was, Jim zoned out.

Bobby slowly slid the chair to avoid squeaking its wheels. "All I got to do is use the super computer then I'll be able to win against all the bad guys 'cause I'll know where their secret hideout is," Bobby whispered under his breath.

He took control of the mouse that sat on the edge of the sink and slid it moving the pointer across the screen. He double, triple and quadruple-clicked, highlighting the boxes arranged in rows, sometimes leaving letters in the boxes, sometimes not.

He began pressing the keys on the keyboard, filling in the spaces that were now empty and replacing the letters where there were letters to be replaced. In a large box at the bottom, he typed *b o b b y*.

The computer did not respond other to change in accordance with Bobby's modifications. "You better tell me where the bad guys are," he whispered, face right up to the screen. "I'm warning you. You better hurry-up and tell me or I'll get you with my attacker." Bobby lifted his still-casted arm. "One... you're gonna be in trouble, two... tell me your secrets 'cause you'll get hurt... two... this is the last time I'm gonna say two. Okay, that's it."

Bobby stood and pushed the chair to the side. It slammed into the wall.

"What are you doing?" Jim turned from the window to see Bobby lift his left leg off the ground and drape it over the top of the metal arm, which attached the monitor to the wall. Jim's lunge was a fraction too late to prevent the swing out into the middle of the room, the loss of grip, and forehead strike on the cold unforgiving floor.

"Mommy!"

Grabbing under his armpits, Bobby was face down on the floor, Jim lifted him into his arms. "It's okay. Whoa... I mean you'll be alright. Just breathe. What you were thinking? Are you okay?"

"No," Bobby whimpered.

"Okay. Calm down," he whispered, stroking his hair.

Through sobs, Bobby responded. "Are they going to have to cut my head off?"

"No Bobby, they won't cut your head off."

"Is my head blood coming out?"

"Your head isn't bleeding."

"Is it broked?"

"Well let me see," said Jim as he looked into Bobby's ear. "Are you broked in there? Nope, not broked."

Bobby laughed.

"Son, why did you do that to the computer." Jim motioned to the monitor but did not, at that point, carefully observe the damage.

"It was... on the names... and spies... I don't know. Daddy. I got hurted again. I must be a really bad boy 'cause I keep getting hurted."

"You're not a bad boy. Sometimes you make bad choices..." Jim lightly touched the newly formed mound on his forehead and asked, "Did you know that you've got a goose egg?"

"What's a goose egg?" mumbled Bobby.

"Hmm. Actually, it's a present from the giant goose. The giant goose is the cousin of the goose I kicked at the zoo. Yep, it was the giant goose that put an egg in your head!"

"Yah, Dad. You kicked the goose. That was so funny."

"It flew for ten miles I kicked it so hard."

"Then it honked at you."

"Yep."

"Yah... awesome."

"Are you feeling better?"

"Uh huh."

"Can I ask you a question?"

"Yah, Dad."

"Why did you hang on the computer?"

"Cause when I...it told me that things... then I would, you know, the bad guys to get them."

"Pardon?"

"Umm, you know, when I talked to the computer, then I could get, you know, to know how to get the guys that were about being bad in the computer."

"But that doesn't explain why you were hanging on the computer."

"Umm, well, when I, it was not telling me, the bad guys, you know, were gonna get away, so I did it."

"Did what?"

"You know."

"Know what? What did you do?"

"I wonked it."

"You *wonked* it? What does wonked it mean?"

"I don't know."

"Did you just make that word up?"

"I don't know."

"Okay, well, you sit on this stool, please tell Daddy if you start to feel sick or sleepy, and I'll try and fix the computer before the doctor comes, okay?"

"Okay."

The fully extended arm hung at an unintended angle towards the middle of the room. Grabbing the monitor, Jim tried to fold the arm back into the wall. No matter how much pressure he applied, it would not go back in. He lifted the computer monitor up into the air, which caused the brace to tear away from the wall. The entire apparatus was now detached and bent, its end resting on the floor. Jim stared at the computer screen, its cord still attached to the desktop, all of the text boxes filled with gibberish.

He turned towards his little boy and opened his mouth. Bobby clutched a blood soaked cloth with his broken arm and pressed against his lip. The goose egg was swelling, there was a tear in his eye and a smile on his face. Jim closed his mouth and pulled a tissue from his pocket. "You've got a real live goose egg in your head!"

"And who put it there, Daddy?"

Jim dabbed at the blood. "The giant goose who's the cousin of the goose I kicked at the zoo of course!"

Bobby laughed hysterically. "That's so funny Dad! How come you broke the computer?"

"I didn't break the computer, you bent the arm when you hung on it."

"But it came off the wall when you pushed the screen up."

"Yes it did. Tell you what. We both broke the computer. What do you think the right thing to do is? Should we run away?"

"No."

"Why not?"

"'Cause it's not nice to break things."

"You're right, but why should we wait and get in trouble?"

"'Cause we broke it."

"You're right buddy. I don't like getting in trouble, but it wouldn't be honest to run away. We'll just have to do what we can to make it right and hopefully it's not too expensive." Jim involuntarily looked at his watch.

When the doctor finally came in, a tall fit man dressed in a knit sweater, sleeves rolled up to the elbows, he looked first at the carnage, then at Jim and then at Bobby. "Wow, looks like you guys had fun in here. You must be Bobby," he said kindly. "My name is Dr. Greds. What happened to you?"

"Daddy broke the computer."

"No... I mean... Uh... I... I was trying to fix it and when I lifted it up, the brace detached from the wall," answered Jim.

Acting as though he'd not heard Jim, Dr. Greds continued, "I thought you came here to get your lip sown up, but you've got a broken arm and a big bruise on your head too."

"I stole Dad's cookies and got my arm broked and my Dad was mad at me when I was on the computer so I bunked my head."

"What he means is..." Jim began but the doctor interrupted.

"And how did you split your lip?"

"I was going to get the bad guys but I jumped off the computer chair, at my house, not here, and hit my lip on the computer desk."

Looking to Jim, the doctor said, "He seems like a pretty active kid."

"That he is. And we've got three others at home."

"I've got three of my own. I can't even come through the door without getting punched in the groin."

"Yep."

"Lucky for you this entire system is being replaced this evening, which means you've actually done us a favor."

"Oh, good," said Jim.

Dr. Greds took the monitor from the chair, "Looks like someone's been doing some typing."

"I'm so sorry," said Jim. "Did he wreck anything?"

"Not permanently. This was Bobby's record. I'll need you to help me by telling me his particulars so we can get his record back to normal."

After three stitches, a confirmation from the doctor there was no concussion and twenty-five minutes with the nurse to get the record fixed up, Jim led Bobby down the hallway with an ice pack attached to his forehead with gauze wrap.

Having helped his son into the van, he hopped into the front seat and started the vehicle. 4:47 p.m.

"Dad?"

"Yes?"

"Remember when you broke the computer?"

Jim opened his mouth then closed it. "I totally smashed it right off the wall."

"You're the strongest Dad ever!"

"I know."

"Hey. Dad. Tell me about the funny goose again." Jim began telling the story about the time he kicked the goose at the zoo as they pulled out of the parking lot.

A Trip to the Movies

"All right, you guys, the first rule is to stay close to Mom and Dad. What is the first rule?"

"Stay close to Mom and Dad!" Grace, Bobby and Stephen chimed in from the back of the van.

"Mama, Dada!" said Jason.

"Okay, the second rule is that you don't do anything stup..."

"Jim!" Marie warned.

Jim stopped dead in his tracks. "Stupid" was one of the words he was not supposed to say. Based on their experience with the use of "whatever," who knew a two year old could be that sarcastic, the use of the word "stupid" by a parent would be especially contagious for their children.

"...the second rule is that you don't do anything bad. What is the second rule?" Marie asked.

"Don't be bad!" Grace, Bobby and Stephen responded.

"Bad boy!" said Jason.

"What are the two rules?" Jim called drill sergeant like.

"Stay close to Mom and Dad and don't be bad!" Grace and Stephen responded. Bobby was staring blankly.

"Bap!" said Jason, apparently deciding he had displayed enough of his new vocabulary for one evening.

"Bobby?" Jim called.

Grace nudged Bobby. "Don't do bad things," replied Bobby.

The rule review session now complete, Jim looked at Marie and asked, "Are you ready?"

"I'm a little nauseous but yes. This should be a lot of fun and I'm really excited for the popcorn. I think it might help." Marie said.

"I was surprised that you were sick this morning. You seem like you have been doing so much better lately."

"I can't complain. If you remember I was sick for all nine months with Grace."

"I remember."

"So this isn't that bad." Marie looked down at her stomach. "I think my body is too used to being pregnant. Everything stretched out so much faster this time."

"You look great."

"Yeah right."

"You do."

"Yah, Mom. If your butt wasn't so big the baby wouldn't have any room to swim around in there," reasoned Grace.

"The baby lives in Mom's butt?" Bobby looked at Stephen and they both exploded with laughter.

Grace turned to Bobby. "Stop it. The baby lives in Mommy's tummy but she goes on trips around Mommy's body when she wants to play. That's why Mom gets so big all over."

"Mommy's not big..." interjected Jim, but was quickly interrupted by Bobby.

"The baby's not a she. She's a boy. And his name is going to be Bobby, like me."

"The baby can't have your name or else it would get in trouble like you every day of the year. Asides it wouldn't be fair if the baby is a boy, right Mom?" asked Grace.

Marie mumbled loudly enough for only Jim to hear, "She calls me fat then wants me to back her up?" The volume immediately increased in response to a fight in the back. "What are you guys doing back there?"

Bobby and Grace froze, his fingers laced in her hair and her nails dug into his chest. "He... he... he," repeated Grace as Bobby rhythmically said, "No... no... no."

Jim turned in his seat. "If you guys don't stop right now, we are not going to the movie." All eyes were wide and all hands were to the side. "This is your last chance. Got it?"

After a long and quiet drive, they finally arrived at the colossal theatre. Passing through the space age automated doors and into the spacious lobby teaming with people, Marie and Jim led the children over to the long line leading to the movie ticket agent and waited.

Confinement by barriers into a single file line, plus the sheer number of people, plus the noise that exceeded normal talking volume, plus the excitement of the theatre equaled a potent chemical reaction in Bobby. Seeing the large crowd gathered, needing and desiring a large crowd, as every performer does to put on a great show, Bobby began his first, and only, routine: the "making the loud unexpected noise" routine. He tilted his head back slightly, opened his mouth to its full extent, closed his eyes and forced the air from his lungs through his vocal cords in pure piccolo style.

His first attempt drew little attention, aside from the woman whose hair stood on end. Her hair was already styled that way, but the shrill sound did cause her to drop her keys.

"Bobby, stop it," Marie said.

Unsatisfied and undaunted, Bobby unleashed the next note with operatic power. People buying snacks on the other end of the large receiving area turned to look in his direction. Before he could blast his siren a third time, his father's hand was clamped on his shoulder. "Why are you screaming?"

Bobby shrugged.

Jim crouched in front of Bobby and whispered, "Do you want to go home right now?"

Bobby's mouth knotted so tightly there was only sufficient space to emit one word. "No."

"I will take you home right now if you do not stop making that sound."

In a mournful tone, Bobby whimpered, "Okay."

While his parents were focused on his now disconsolate older brother, Stephen chatted to the fabric tape that provided a guide for the serpentine queue of people leading up to the ticket wicket, "Are you where this thing comes from?"

A gentle-faced woman on the other side of the fabric strip, accompanied by a miniature version of her, answered, "I beg your pardon?"

Oblivious to the woman, he wasn't being rude, he just wasn't talking to her, Stephen continued his conversation with the metal pole. "May I play with you?"

The pole did not respond.

Stephen grabbed the plastic end of the fabric divider and slid it out of its slot. Much to his delight, it zipped from the first pole and retracted like a measuring tape does when the lock is taken off. Stephen did not notice it whipping the miniature version of the woman across the face as it was drawn into the pole.

"Stephen Tanner!"

Startled by the mélange of alarm and anger in his mother's voice, Stephen toppled face first into the metal divider. "Wah! Ouch, ouch."

Marie picked Stephen up and stood him on his feet. "What are you doing?" Stephen cried and said nothing. "Can you pick him up please?"

Jim released Bobby, scooped up Stephen then helped Marie up from her knees with his free hand. The dueling cries from the two bawling children by this point had drawn the attention of at least eighty-seven percent of the patrons of the theatre. The other thirteen percent were dealing with their own children.

Marie turned to the woman consoling her child. "I'm so sorry about your daughter. Is she okay?"

"If you watched your children more closely this wouldn't have happened," the gentle faced woman snapped back.

Marie clenched her teeth. "He didn't mean to hurt your daughter."

"Well he did. How many kids do you have? Maybe that's your problem." Some people looked away shocked, others nodded.

"I have said sorry to you, and I meant it. I'm not sure what else you want from me." Thankfully at that moment the line shifted, separating Marie's family and that of the mother, never to cross paths in that line again.

"Are you okay?" an older woman next to Marie asked.

"I'm fine thank you. Will you excuse me please? Jim I'll be right back." Marie excused herself from the line.

"Where are you going?" asked Jim.

"I'll be right back."

Jim turned from his wife to the sobbing boy with the red mark on his cheek. "Stephen, what happened?"

"I..." he began gasping "asked..." hiccupping he continued "if I... could play with it."

"What? Play with what?"

"The... thingy."

"What thingy are you talking about?"

"That one..." he said pointing to the metal pole.

"Okay, now get a hold of yourself. Breathe. That's right breathe. I want you to stand right next to Daddy. Okay?"

"O-kay." Jim placed Stephen on the floor.

Jason sat on the floor on the other side of his father. Directly behind his father was a pair of most interesting feet. They were bare except for a rubber sole and a strap over the foot. The long yellowish toenails extended beyond the toe like miniature diving boards. The odor emanating from these feet stung Jason's nose. He shifted so he was within arm's length of the foot and touched the furry toe very gently. As he moved in for the taste test his mother interrupted him.

"Jason. No," she ordered, scooping him up.

"Where did you go?" asked Jim.

"I went to the concession to buy the little girl a treat."

"And how did that go?"

"It's amazing how candy can improve the relationship of both adults and children."

"Next please," called the cashier.

The Tanners stepped up to her, except for Grace, who eyed her father from head to toe. "Dad, your pants don't match your shirt."

The entire family froze. Even the boys looked surprised at Grace's terrible timing.

"Your Dad's pants do match his shirt," said Marie. "What is going on with you guys? Are you trying to ruin this trip? Do you want to go home?"

"No," moaned the children.

"Then will you please be good like we asked you," reminded Jim.

"Yes," moaned the children.

Marie was about to address the cashier when Grace said, "But you said that brown and blue don't go together."

Marie inhaled and exhaled slowly. "It's a little different with blue jeans. It's okay to wear a brown shirt with jeans."

"Oh. Okay, Mommy," said Grace as she leaned into her father and clutched his hand. Jim sighed.

"Which movie are you folks going to see?" the cashier asked as the family turned its attention to her.

"Canadian Wilderness Adventure featuring Goober Gopher," said Marie.

"For how many."

"Two adults and four children," said Marie.

"Whoa. Are all these kids your kids?"

Marie looked to Jim. He answered, "Yes."

In the Theatre

"Why is it so dark? I can't see with my eyes," Stephen said as the family entered the dimly lit room. Rows of chairs cascaded down the sloped floor towards the humongous screen.

"Don't worry, Stephen, I've got you," Marie assured.

"Let's sit here," Bobby said, pointing to the front row.

"No way. I want to sit back there," Grace retorted, pointing to the back of the theatre.

"Look you guys, I am not going to get into this right now. You guys can figure out where you'd like to sit and you'd better be quick because if you wait too long we're not going to be able to sit anywhere," said Jim, his arms folded.

"I'll be your friend if you let me sit in the back," sang Grace.

"No."

"Fine. I'm not your friend then."

"That is not what your dad meant by working it out. Since you can't work this out and be kind to each other, we'll just sit in the middle," said Marie as she motioned to the middle of theatre.

"Aw!" moaned Bobby and Grace in unison.

"Well if you've got a problem with it, you two get together and figure out what you want to do," said Jim. By this point they were causing a traffic jam, the flow of theatre patrons being stopped by the Tanner family plug.

"I wanna sit at the front."

"I want to sit at the back."

"Fine. We are going to sit in the middle and if I hear you whine, I will take you home," warned Marie.

"Okay," they said, triggering the filing of the family, duck and duckling-like, thirteen rows up from the bottom of the theatre. Marie was left to settle the kids in their seats while Jim left for pop and popcorn.

"This is a nice theatre - it's very dark - my feet are getting stuck on the floor - what are those people's names - what movie are we seeing - when will we get our drinks - can I have some popcorn - can I sit next to Bobby - why are you giving that to Grace - are there bats in the theatre?" said Stephen in one breath.

His questions not immediately answered, Stephen patted his seat until he had his mother's attention. Once she had finished with Jason, Marie held the seat down for him. No sooner had Stephen grabbed the front corners of the chair, than Marie was compelled by garbled arguing to move down the row to intervene in a Bobby-Grace battle. Stephen pushed off the ground and slithered himself onto the seat à la Sneaky the Snake. He got up onto his knees, rotated towards the humongous screen and leaned back, unfolding his legs over the edge of his seat. Once his little backside hit the back of the seat, it began to close on him, trash compactor like, folding him in half, driving his feet to his face, which fortunately was not an issue because Stephen just happened to be freakishly flexible. "Help Momma!"

"Grace, your brother is not a rotten apple. Bobby, do not touch your sister again."

"Help, Help, HELP!" Stephen cried.

"Whoa... Grace take Jason." Marie dropped Jason on Grace's lap, sprinted past the three empty chairs and pressed down on the front of Stephen's seat. "Are you okay?"

"I guess I smelt like hot dogs."

"What?"

"The chair was hungry so it eated me. When I smell hot dogs I feel hungry too."

Marie stifled her laughter. "You mean... why hot dogs?"

"Yeah, I think I felt its teeth biting my forehead, but I'm okay, don't worry about me, I'm tough."

Marie doubled over, breathlessly striving for air she needed to expel her laughter.

Returning to his pregnant wife breathless and doubled over, Jim placed the food on the floor and put his hand on her back. "Are you okay?"

"He wants... hot dog."

"What? Who wants a hot dog? I don't want to go back for more treats... Is the baby okay? Are you laughing or crying?"

"Laughing."

"What's so funny?" he asked.

"Stephen … eaten … chair …" Marie blurted between giggles.

"Stephen ate the chair?"

Marie shook her head. "The chair… the chair ate him," she said, wiping the tears from her eyes.

"Okay? So who wants the hot dog?"

"No. Stephen thought he tasted like a hot dog."

"Oh. Hmm. I guess you had to be there."

"I guess so. I'm going to go get some booster seats for the kids… hot dog. Her laughter rang through the room.

Jim inspected his little boy's mouth. "Why did you eat the chair? That's so gross."

"No Dad, the chair eated me. Like this." Stephen was again folded, then unfolded by his dad.

"I see," said Jim. Marie returned with four booster seats.

Grace, however, refused the one intended for her by saying, "Mom, I'm big enough now I don't need that, and what happens if my friends see me?"

"Let me know if you change your mind," answered Marie.

Finally everyone was settled and the previews began.

"I want popcorn!" shouted Bobby.

"Me too," cried Stephen.

"Bap," Jason hooted happily.

"Can I please be first. It's so hard being the only girl. Being first with the popcorn would make it so much easier," said Grace in a strained voice. Without the assistance of the booster seat, her chair was threatening to swallow her.

Marie ducked her head so she would not obstruct the view of the screen for the other patrons. Napkins tucked securely under her left armpit,

Marie crept from chair to chair creating a paper napkin lining within the drink holder to the right of each child. Once prepared, she took a large handful from the bag of popcorn in her left hand and dumped it into each receptacle.

Jim sat next to Grace and placed his right leg over the front of her chair. Grace's shaking ceased. Relieved, she asked, "Dad, do you remember how last week I told you that Millie had seen the movie and was making life so difficult for me?"

Jim nodded cautiously.

"I'm so glad we're watching this movie so that she can't do that again," said Grace.

"Do what again?"

"Dad, don't you remember?"

"Umm. No."

"But it was so important to me."

"I'm sorry sweetie. Sometimes my memories escape out of my bald spot. I can't do anything about it."

"Why don't you wear a hat then?"

"Hats aren't good enough for it. You need hair but my head doesn't like hair where my bald spot is any more so you'll have to tell me what happened."

"Well she said the reason I didn't get to see the movie was because my bed time was early enough to be for a baby."

"Oh. I'm glad she won't be able to do that again."

"Me too, Daddy," said Grace as she tucked her arm in his.

Now that everyone had popcorn, the communal drinks made their way up and down the row, each child taking as much or as little as he or she desired. Jim and Marie sat bookend around the boys and Grace sat to Jim's right. The tenseness of the events leading up to this moment fading, the only sound coming from the children being the munching of popcorn, and the darkness of the room setting the stage for imagination to meld with the film, the couple gave an air high five and turned their attention away from the kids. Momentarily.

"I really gotta go to the bathroom," announced Bobby as he leapt from his chair.

"Are you serious? The opening credits haven't even finished yet," Jim stated.

"Yes," whimpered Bobby, knees knocking, hands over his groin, panic in the eyes: the pee-pee dance. Jim grabbed his desperate son by the hand and hastily escorted him out of the theatre. They returned five minutes later, having missed the first few minutes of the movie.

"Marie, what did I miss?" whispered Jim.

"Sneaky the Snake is a world-class luger."

"Oh." Jim settled in.

At first, the bright flashing lights on the massive screen greatly held Jason's attention, but once his eyes adjusted to the light, he could see there were also all sorts of things to do in the theater. He slid himself to the end of his booster seat using the left cheek, right cheek, bum-scoot method. Marie slid him back. He tried again. His mother slid him back again.

"No," said Jason, pushing Marie's hand to the side.

"I don't want you running all over the theatre."

Jason screamed.

"Fine. I'll let you down but you can only play right here, okay?"

"Yep." Once he had bum scooted to the end of his seat, he flipped himself over and began searching for the floor with his feet to no avail. He lowered himself a little more but his feet still did not touch the floor. He kicked and screamed, "Mama!"

Marie gently placed her hands on either side of Jason's torso and carefully lowered him to the floor. "Shhh. You're being too loud."

Now safely on the floor, Jason paced back and forth, determining the limits of his play area. Unable to lift Daddy's legs, getting a *no* from Mom each time he tried to lift hers, it was clear his boundaries ended with their legs. Apparently satisfied with how much room he had to explore, he turned his attention to playing.

"Hey!"

Jason, with his fingers spread wide apart, was hitting the woman in front of him as though he were repeatedly spiking a volleyball and her head was the volleyball.

Marie snatched Jason. "Don't hit."

"Okay," whimpered Jason.

"Say sorry."

"Sawwy."

"I'm so sorry ma'am."

"It's all right."

Grace quietly stood, shuffled over to Marie and whispered, "Can you take me to the bathroom?"

Lifting Jason into her arms, walking back towards Jim, placing him in Jim's lap, Marie whispered, "I'm going to take Grace to the bathroom."

As soon as Marie and Grace disappeared out of the theatre, Stephen shouted, "I have to go to the bathroom!" Neither Bobby nor Jason could be left on their own. Jim poked Bobby, signaled for him to come, stood up with Jason in his right arm and held Stephen's hand. All four of them made their way to the boy's bathroom.

The configuration of the rows of clean white urinals on one side and graffiti free stalls on the other side presented Jim with a problem. "Daddy's got to help Stephen in the bathroom. Bobby, will you please watch your little brother and make sure he doesn't play in the toilets?"

"Yep," responded Bobby.

"Please watch your brother."

"I will."

Jim helped Stephen onto the toilet.

Thud

thud thud

"What's going on out there?"

thud thud thud.

Creek.

"Answer me."

Thud thud.

Splash.

"Bobby are you watching your brother?"

"I don't know where... oh, he's at the toilet right beside you."

"Jason, Jason, Jason, can you hear Daddy, Jason? Don't play in the water. Don't play. Don't play in the water! Bobby, is your brother playing in the toilet?"

"He's not playing in the toilet," replied Bobby.

"Oh good, can you take him away from the potty, please."

"Okay," answered Bobby. Thud, thud, thud, thud, thud. "Come on, Jason."

"No," Jason screeched.

"Daddy said so."

"No." Smack.

"Daddy, Jason hitted me," cried Bobby.

"Okay. Don't let him play in the water, I'll be right there."

"You aren't going to let me fall in the toilet, are you Dad? My bum bum's too small to sit on the seat if you don't hold me," said a worried Stephen.

"I won't leave, but are you almost done?" asked Jim.

Smack, smack, smack. "Jason keeps hitting me!"

"Umm, I'm not almost done yet, Dad. Just a little more," answered Stephen.

"No!" screamed Jason. Thud, thud, thud, thud, thud.

"You've got to finish now, Stephen. Bobby, are you still with Jason?"

"But I'm not done yet," answered Stephen.

"But he keeps hitting me," protested Bobby.

Jim pulled away from Stephen. "Whoa, Dad. I almost fell in. Don't let go. I don't want to go in the toilet."

"Okay then, pull up your pants and go wash your hands," said Jim. Splash, splash, splash. "Hurry, your brother is playing in the toilet."

"But I'm not finished yet," said Stephen.

"Can you please…"

"I'm done Dad," announced Stephen.

"Great," Jim whisked Stephen off the toilet, tugged his pants up and left him to straighten them. Jim rounded the corner to Jason licking the side of the toilet bowl.

"Why did you… I don't understand why… that is so disgusting," mumbled Jim as he brought Jason to the sink and scrubbed the struggling boy's face with soap and water. "You can't do that, don't do that again!"

"Do what?" Bobby replied.

"No, I'm talking to your brother. Why didn't you watch him?"

"'Cause he was hitting me, Daddy. Don't you 'memember?" replied Bobby.

"Just go wait by the door, okay?"

Having now missed the classic *Sneaky the Snake and Goober Gopher misunderstanding results in a conflict on which to move the plot forward* scene and the *ah hah Goober Gopher moment,* a result of two additional Bobby bathroom trips, when Bobby shouted for the fourth time that he needed to go to the bathroom, Jim offered to take him... but he was in no hurry.

No doubt struggling with the legitimate question as to why they had brought their children to the theatre, Jim sauntered while Bobby pee pee danced all the way to the bathroom. Another film had let out between bathroom trip three and four and a group of boys and men with terrible aim had made their disgusting mark on the bathroom, and in particular on the toilet seats. Bobby flung the first door open to a repulsive seat. "Bobby you can't sit on that seat. There isn't enough toilet paper to make that clean."

"But Dad, I have to go so bad," he responded.

"Let's try the next one over, okay son?"

"But I really have to go."

Jim led the boy to the next stall, which to his horror was far worse than the first. "You're going to have to stand and go."

"I don't want to pee standing up," Bobby responded, his voice echoing in the empty room.

"You are a big boy and it's a lot of fun. See you can stand up and go pee in there."

"No."

"It's really easy and you can pretend you're shooting the water."

"No. I don't want to."

"Tell you what. Just start by pulling down your pants."

"Can you help me?"

"Can't you do it by yourself?"

Tugging frantically at his pants, Bobby cried, "I can't."

Jim stepped into the stall with Bobby and pulled Bobby's pants down. "Now turn and face the toilet."

"I'm too scared. I wanna sit down on the toilet."

"Bobby, that seat is disgusting. I don't want you to get someone else's pee on you."

"Okay," he whined. He didn't move.

Jim turned Bobby towards the toilet. "Okay now. Just shoot the water with your pee. You're really going to like it." No sooner had the words escaped Jim's lips than Bobby spun back towards his father and, unable to resist any longer, urinated on his father's jeans.

"You... why did... you were standing..." Jim walked away from his son. Hesitating momentarily at the exit, he passed by and headed for the paper towels. He methodically wiped himself off and tossed the soiled paper in the garbage, looking as though he was having a silent angry conversation with himself. The conversation apparently complete, he exhaled and grabbed more paper towel. "Here. Clean yourself up."

"Okay," moaned Bobby. Loud talking indicated their movie had finished and they were not going to be alone for much longer. Jim snatched the paper towel from Bobby, wiped him off and escaped from the bathroom with his son.

Marie, Grace, Stephen and Jason stood in the middle of the now bustling hallway. "Is everything okay," asked Marie.

"Not ready to talk about it yet," responded Jim. The walk to the parking lot was tense and hurried. This silence continued as everyone climbed into the van.

"What did you do to Dad?" whispered Grace.

"I don't know," responded Bobby.

"He hasn't said anything to anybody since we met you guys in the hallway. You must have done something."

"Maybe he's mad at you, Grace."

"I don't think so."

"Uh huh, he's mad at you!"

"No, he's mad at you!"

"You guys should be quiet," said Jim.

Stephen, who had not said a word until now, did not take the cue. "Dad, how come your bald spot's all red?"

"I don't know why my bald spot is red."

"Is it because you're mad? Why are you so mad, Dad?" Stephen persisted.

"Well, I guess Daddy is a little frustrated that he paid money for a movie ticket for himself and for Mommy and neither of us saw much of the movie."

"Why didn't you see much?" asked Stephen.

"Hmm, let's see. Bobby how many times did you go to the bathroom at the theatre?"

"I don't know."

"Quite a few. And Grace how many times did you go?"

"Once."

"Stephen, how many times did you go?"

"One time, Daddy."

"When you add up the time it took to take you guys to the bathroom, Mommy saw about twenty-eight minutes of the movie and Daddy saw about seventeen minutes," he said, exaggerating just a little.

"Oh," said Stephen, momentarily satisfied. Then another thought struck him. "How come your pants are wet? I saw when you were walking that your pants were wet."

"Why don't you ask Bobby?" Jim said quietly.

"Bobby," Stephen began, "how come Daddy's pants are wet?"

"He got pee on them. I peed on them."

Silence reigned for the next few moments until, true to form, Stephen spoke. "I guess we need a new rule."

"A new rule?" asked Marie.

"Yeah. Stay close to Mom and Dad, don't be bad, and don't pee on Dad or he'll be sad."

In spite of himself, Jim chuckled. Stephen, delighted with his dad's response, excitedly repeated, "don't pee on Dad or he'll be sad," and punctuated it with triumphant laughter.

"I think that's a great rule Stephen," said Marie.

"Agreed," said Jim.

"I'm sorry I peed on you, Dad," Bobby offered contritely.

"Just remember the new rule for next time, alright?"

"Don't pee on Dad or he'll be sad. Okay, Daddy."

Poor Stephen

"It's probably a million thousand hundred days 'til Saturday," said Stephen, still tucked under his covers on the bottom bunk bed. Wiping the left over sleep glue from his eyes, he shouted, "Is it Saturday yet?"

"Mom, where's my backpack?" shouted Grace from downstairs.

"It's by the front door where you left it. Bobby, you need to hurry up or you're going to be late for school," said Marie as she scrambled to get the crew out the door before 7:53 a.m., which would give her enough travel time to get them to school before the bell at 8:05 a.m.

"Why do Grace and Bobby get to go to school without me?" moaned Stephen, the frantic jabbering from downstairs ever audible. "What's wrong with me? Dad says I'm a smart guy so how come I got to stay home? Jason can play with all my stuff like he always wants to if I go to school. I want to go to school. I'm smart enough. I really am smart enough. It doesn't matter if I'm four."

"Bobby, you have five minutes to finish your toast," warned Marie.

"Why doesn't anybody listen to me?" Stephen pedal kicked his covers off and slid out of bed. Frowning, he skipped down the hallway, slid down the stairs and danced his way to the kitchen. When he reached the breakfast table, he sat down in his chair, folded his arms, placed them on the table and rested his chin on them. "Humph."

His older siblings were far too interested in the back of the cereal boxes to notice their little brother. He tried again. "Humph."

"Stephen, what would you like for breakfast?" Marie asked as she walked back into the kitchen.

Glaring at his mother, he gripped the table in front of him and shouted, "I want cereal!"

"Excuse me? I am not your slave."

"But you were acknoring me all morning so you better get me some cereal... please." All was still at breakfast time, the eyes of his siblings fixed on their bowls.

"You will not talk to me that way. Go and sit on the stairs."

"But, I said please."

"It was what you said before the please that's the problem. Go now!"

"But, I..."

"Stephen Tanner, I don't know what has gotten into you. If you don't go now you are going to regret it."

His face crying with no tears or sound, Stephen slid his chair just enough to slip out and tip toed out of the kitchen and into the living room. He hovered next to the stairs, half-standing, half-sitting, until his mother shouted, "You sit down right now or so help me."

Stephen sat. He started by placing his head in his hands, which transformed into lying on his side, which developed into moaning and weeping, which descended into loud apologizing; the three minutes passed agonizingly slow for Stephen. He started to stand when two year old Jason came out of the kitchen. "Hi."

"You're not 'posed to talk to me. I'm a bad boy."

Jason toddled over and put his hand on his brother's leg. "Ba boy?"

"Cause I yelled at Mom."

"Play?"

"I can't play. I'm in time out."

"Oh," said Jason as he sat next to his brother. "Me ba boy."

"No, you're a good boy Jason."

"No, ba boy," he said smacking his brother playfully on the shoulder.

"Oh, you're going to hit me are you?" Stephen said, dog paddling his arms.

Taking the hint, Jason mimicked his older brother, lightly making contact with the tips of Stephen's fingers. He giggled insanely.

"Are you ready to be a good boy, Stephen?" asked Marie, frantically trying to put together the lunches on the kitchen counter.

"Yes, Mom," laughed Stephen.

"Okay. Why don't you sit down at the table and I'll bring you breakfast?"

"Okay." Hand in hand, the brothers walked back into the kitchen.

"See, Mommy? Me and Jason are best buddies."

"I'm so glad you are getting along but what do you need to say?"

"Sorry, Mommy."

"That's better. Here's your breakfast." Marie placed a bowl of cereal on the table.

"Thank you."

"I have a surprise for you today." All four children turned towards their mother. But she looked only at Stephen.

"What is it?"

"I've arranged for a new friend to come over and play," said Marie.

"A friend?" Stephen began with a giggle, "What's his name, where will we play, is he friendly, what will we play ..."

"Aw, that's not fair," cried Bobby. Grace's facial expression matched her brother's whine.

"You get to go to school and play with your friends every day. It's only fair that…"

"Hey, Mom, how many do I have to count before my new buddy gets here?"

"He's not coming until after the kids are in school, honey. You're going to have to be patient."

"But how many is that?"

"After the kids are in school."

Marie should have clarified that some time would pass between them dropping Grace and Bobby off at school and Stephen's new friend arriving. The minute the bell rang the barrage commenced.

"How old is my buddy?"

"Stephen, he's…"

"Is he twenty-four? That's almost as old as you, Mom, and you're really old. Probably the oldest person I know, except Papa Tanner." Papa Tanner was ninety-two.

"I'm not that old…"

"Does my new buddy got big muscles? Like this," he said striking a pose as they climbed in the van.

"Stephen, I…"

"I bet he's a super hero. He's got a cape and boots and sword and gun and… and… and… special underwear so you don't got to go to the bathroom when you're chasing bad guys."

"Do you mean a diaper?"

"No, a superhero doesn't wear a diaper. They're super pants. The poopoos and the peepees just get eated up by the super pants."

"Oh, tell me more."

"That means that when the bad guys got to go potty my buddy just uses his super sticky spray to trap them."

"Stephen, you have to realize…"

"Ha ha ha. He can fly. I knew it. He's gonna take me on an amazing adventure to save the town from the wicked Imp. Just like Oliver. Except I can't talk to plants but I'll be able to fly and he doesn't got to go to the bathroom so we'll be able to beat the Imp, Professor Stouch and the Venus fly trap."

"What are you talking about?"

"You know, like from the game on your touch pad."

"You mean my iPhone?"

"So when he comes, you got to get us a super snack. He's really tough so you might have to cook a whole buffalo head and give him the brains for his muscles. Oh and Jell-O and pizza and ice cream and pancakes."

"Is that all?"

"And pancakes," he echoed, stepping out of the van and walking toward the house.

"Are you finished?"

"Finished what?"

"Listing the things that you want."

"What things?"

"You were talking about all the things you and your super buddy were going to eat."

"I wasn't talking to you about that. Just talking to myself."

Simon

Ding dong.

Stephen's short legs carried him double time from the kitchen through the living room where he scaled the arm of the couch only to somersault onto the cushions, which he bounded off, landing next to his mother who had walked steadily from the dishwasher to the front door.

"Do you have to go to the bathroom?" asked Marie.

"Nope," answered Stephen.

"Then why are you dancing around like that?"

"I'm just so excited to meet my super friend."

Marie opened the front door.

A woman with blond hair and smiley eyes stood hand in hand with a little boy who was even shorter than Stephen. "Hi, Janice. Come on in."

"I'd love to Marie, but I've got to run. Thank you so much for taking Simon." Janice knelt next to Simon. "You be a good boy, okay?"

The boy nodded. He had short hair, chocolate colored eyes and rosy red cheeks. He looked like the type of boy you might see on a 1950s box of cereal. His mother planted a kiss on his cheek, waived good bye to Marie, looked longingly at her son for a brief moment then was off the step. As soon as Marie closed the door, Simon's eyes were filled with tears.

"This guy is not a superhero," Stephen said.

"Stephen!" Calmer, Marie continued, "This is Simon."

"But why's he crying? Where's his chest hair?"

"He's crying because he misses his Mom. Come here." Simon snuggled into Marie.

"I thought he was going to be able to throw me in the air and stuff like that. Daddy said you gots to have lots of chest hair to be tough."

"Be nice."

"Fine. I guess it's okay that you're pretty wimpy. I'll throw you..."

"Stephen."

Taking his mother's cue, Stephen grabbed Simon's hand. "Come on buddy, let's go play upstairs in my room. Bobby's not home so we can play with his stuff."

"Make sure you clean up any mess you make."

A muscle bound action figure, in hand, Stephen asked Simon, who sat cross-legged with a stuffed frog in his lap "What do you like to do? Are you a super-fast runner? Do you like spaceships?"

"Ey pla gams otsi, ey runs fastas liitnen..." Simon responded.

"What? I mean, pardon me?"

"Dyu wann go otsi, an runs fastas liitnen wid mi?"

Stephen carefully placed his toy on the ground, walked over to his friend and put his hand on the boy's shoulder. "Are you on the wrong channel?" This would seem a strange question but yesterday, while watching Sneaky the Snake with Jason, a brotherly battle for control of the remote control resulted in a new station with nothing but garbled words. Simon sounded like he was on the wrong channel.

Simon shrugged Stephen's hand off his shoulder and continued bouncing the frog.

"Do you like birthdays? I like birthdays. I'm three years old. I want another birthday so I can be four. How old are you?" Simon opened his mouth to answer, but before he could utter the unintelligible response, Stephen put his hand on Simon's mouth. "All I need is to have a birthday and then I'll be older. Think, think, think. How am I going to have a birthday?"

"Brtday sawn," answered Simon.

"You're right, super buddy. Happy Birthday song!" Stephen stood up. "Stand up, buddy, 'cause then we can sing so much louder. Come on. Stand up!"

Simon seemed pleased at this suggestion and began to sing the song. Stephen joined in.

"Happy Birthday to me, I have to go pee, if I don't get older, I will go back to three." Stephen scaled the desk and looked out the window. "The school bus isn't here to pick me up yet." He jumped down and dashed across the hall. He angled his head in the mirror. "I don't got a bald spot." He ran back, sat down, pulled out the neckline of his shirt, looked at his chest and proclaimed, "Sing again, it's not working. I don't got any chest hair. Sing and don't stop, don't stop!"

Simon sang louder. Stephen felt his chin. "Not even a wizard beard yet. There must be something wrong. Maybe it's 'cause we don't got no birthday cake. But we ated cake yesterday and I'm still little. Okay Simon, you can stop singing now. Stop!"

Simon's happy yet practically unintelligible singing stopped abruptly.

"Lash plai," said Simon.

"Fine." Stephen went to his closet, took out some building blocks and sat down with his friend. The tower never got higher than three blocks high before the cookie box boy swatted it, sending the blocks across the room. "Do you have to do that?"

Simon nodded and placed a block on top of another.

"I ated cake, but I didn't get older." The blocks crashed across the room. "But when I ated a birthday cake I got older...the candles! Hah!" Stephen exclaimed triumphantly as he hurried out of the room.

Simon hardly noticed that his playmate had left him. He was wholly focused on the tower he was about to swat.

Stephen casually walked past his mother as she tidied the living room.

"Is everything okay?" asked Marie.

"Yep."

"Are you guys having fun?"

"Uh huh! We're playing happy birthday and I'm gonna be four!" Stephen responded.

"Where are you going?"

"Umm. I... just want to get a snack for Simon and me."

"I guess that's okay. Only one each though."

"Okay."

Racing past his mother, he grabbed the barbecue lighter from the drawer and shoved it into his pocket. It didn't fit. He removed it and slid it into his underwear, the handle supported by the waistband and the barrel extending out the leg hole. He carefully made his way back into the living room.

"Why are you walking like that?" asked Marie.

"Like what?"

"Like you've been riding a horse for three hours."

"Oh, umm, I was pretending I was riding a horse." Stephen adjusted his waistband.

"What do you have..." Just then Jason fell off the couch, slamming his head against the floor. Stephen slipped up the stairs while his mother tended to his younger brother.

He returned to a weeping Simon. "What's wrong my buddy?"

"I dint nowd wer you is."

"I'm here. Look at this," said Stephen unsheathing his older-maker.

"A gun?"

"Nope. Magic fire starter. See." Stephen pulled the trigger and a small flame appeared.

Simon put his hands up. "Carfa Steben."

Stephen released the trigger. "I want to get older, so we're going to have a birthday party. Your job is to sing happy birthday okay. I just need to find some candles. Don't you want to get older too? You can if you are in my birthday party."

"Habby birfday ta you."

"Wait. Not yet. Where's some candles?"

Stephen looked around his room. "Dinky cars ... nope, stuffed bear Binky ... nope, muscle man Jake ... nope." He sat on his bed, holding the fire starter in one hand, and twisting the yarn tassels that hung from the edge with his other.

"Steben, canda," said Simon pointing at the yarn between his fingers, as he was now sitting on the bed, copying his new friend. Stephen had been twisting two strings together until they were wound tightly enough that they would unwind if released.

"What do you mean?"

Simon released his strings and pointed at Stephen's. "Canda!"

Stephen gripped the lighter tightly. "The strings on my blanket are like candles. You are a great friend Simon."

"Tank oo."

Stephen pressed the trigger. "Let's do this right. One, two, three... Happy birthday to me, happy birthday to me, happy birthday to me, happy birthday to me, happy birthday to me, come on Simon, you sing too ..." A narrow strand of smoke lofted up from the yarn. A small flame appeared then Stephen blew it out. "Now I'm four! I can feel my muscles growing. If I was five, I'd be even stronger."

He pulled the trigger and held it to the smoldering strings. They started on fire. Stephen moved to some untwisted strings. "Maybe I should be older. I'll start more fire then blow more out then I'll be so old… I'll be fifteen!"

Two independent fires grew as Stephen moved to another set of strings. "No Steben. Bad Steben. Stoppit."

"I'm gonna be a million years old," shouted Stephen maniacally.

Marie sat on the living room floor, between the couches and the television, playing with Jason. "Hi. Is Jason there?" asked Marie, holding the phone to her ear.

"Momma here," said Jason into his shoe.

"Are you talking on the phone Jas... Simon what's wrong?" asked Marie. Simon ran at full speed directly towards her.

With a panicked look he shouted, "Hers bad!"

"Pardon me?" Marie asked.

"Hers bad ouchy," Simon shrieked his arms swinging over his head.

"Slow down, Simon. I don't understand."

Simon grabbed Marie's hand and pulled her towards the stairs. She got up from the floor, lifted Jason into her arms and headed for the stairs. "Come now! Come now! Fire!"

"Fire?" Marie asked.

Simon nodded.

"Simon, stay here with Jason." She placed Jason on the floor and ran up the stairs. Bobby and Stephen's door was closed. She threw it open. Stephen was frantically blowing at the flames that had spread from the yarn to the blanket.

"Get out of this room now." Stephen ran from the room. Marie rushed to the bathroom, grabbed a bucket filled it with water and rushed back to douse the flames. Three buckets of water later, the flames had been completely extinguished.

Marie walked back down the stairs. Stephen stood quietly facing the stairs as the other two boys watched a television program.

"I can't believe you would do such a dumb thing. Do you know you could have burnt yourself, our house and maybe even killed someone? I have raised you better than this. Do you want me to have this baby early? What do you have to say for yourself?"

Stephen kicked at the floor. "I turned on the TV so the boys would be okay."

"Stephen! I'm going to... you just... you could have burned our house down and seriously hurt yourself. Fire does not go in your room. You are never to play with fire anywhere. Do you understand?"

"Yes."

"Do you? I can't believe you would do that. Haven't I taught you to behave better than this? Is this the way you're going to act if you have a friend over?"

"No."

"Why did you do this?"

"I wanted to be four," Stephen mumbled.

"What? What did you say?"

"I wanted to be four."

"So you want to be four, huh? If you keep starting fires like that you might not make it to four! Since four is so important you can spend the next year in your room thinking about how nice it will be to be four. In fact, why stop at four? You are in a time out until you are eighteen. Go to your room. Right, you can't do that because you destroyed your room. Go to my room."

"But I want to play with Simon."

Marie stepped towards Stephen. "No. You will be going to your room. Now." Stephen ran for the stairs.

Fully briefed on his return, Jim went to Stephen's room. The bed spread was no longer wet, nor the floor, but the smell of burnt fabric and campfire permeated the space. He turned and crossed the hallway to his room to find the small boy sitting meekly on the bed, his eyes closed, a sound like the purring of a cat emanating from him. Jim lightly touched his arm. Stephen lifted his head slightly and struggled to open his eyes. Before Jim could say anything, Stephen looked up sadly at his father and asked, "Am I eighteen yet? This is taking a really long time."

The Great Escape

"Here he comes," whispered Bobby to himself as Noah Jones, a runny-nosed, over-sized kindergartener, started towards him from the other side of the classroom. He ignored Noah and continued drawing.

"That's a very nice picture of our classroom," Mrs. Bredin said to Bobby.

His kindergarten teacher, a rail thin woman, dressed in a purple blouse and dark blue slacks, hovered over Bobby's shoulder on the side opposite Noah. "Umm, Mrs. Bredin can you..." Bobby looked up but the teacher was making her way to another round table populated by other kindergarteners.

Kindergarten was held in an open room, divided only by the small colored tables that made up the children's play stations each with its own separate theme. The teacher's desk was at the back of the room facing the colored tables. It was covered with trinkets. Children's coats covered half of the wall behind the teacher's desk, their outdoor shoes neatly placed below.

"Yeah, nice picture of the classroom, Baby" Noah sneered.

Bobby whipped to face the un-wiped nose. "My name is not Baby, No-Duh!"

Without warning, Noah swiped Bobby's glue stick and wiped it down the sleeve of Bobby's favorite Goober Gopher shirt and onto his arm. Noah bent over and whispered into Bobby's ear, "That's what you get for calling me a name, Baby."

"This is what you get for being a... a... snotty fat face." Bobby brought his elbow back, clenched his fist and drove it into the fleshy part of Noah's belly, doubling his foe over, sending the glue stick to the floor where it made two full spins then stopped motionless next to the pink station.

Mrs. Bredin charged towards him. "Robert Tanner! Name calling and hitting has no place in this classroom. Do you understand?"

"But... but... Noah called me Baby and he put glue on my arm and on my t-shirt and he took my glue and left his station before he's 'posed to."

"Come here Noah. Bobby, you will apologize to Noah and then you will be sitting in the corner."

"But he..."

"Do you need to go to the office?" asked the teacher. Noah stood just enough behind her that she couldn't see the booger besmirched smirk.

"No, but he's... just look..."

"Then you must apologize."

"Sorry, No-Duh," said Bobby, emphasizing the *duh*.

The teacher silenced Bobby's classmates' giggles with a glance. "Do I need to contact your mother?"

"No."

"Then what do you have to say for yourself?"

Bobby kicked the ground lightly. "Sorry Noah."

"Thank you. Now you shake his hand." Still behind Mrs. Bredin, Noah slowly and purposefully used the palm of his hand to smear the undisturbed boogers hanging from his nose. The liquid glistened on his outstretched hand. "Shake it."

"But he just..."

"Do you need to go to the office?" The sound of *oo* coming from the other kids only punctuated her point. Bobby robotically held out his hand. Noah practically lunged in to grip the offering, leaving much of the mucous on Bobby's fingers and hand. Bobby wiped his hand on the side of his pants and said, "Gross."

"That's it. Go sit in the corner." Mrs. Bredin nudged Bobby from the spot where he was rooted, ignoring his "But... but..."

Neither his pleading looks as he plodded along nor his slouched shoulders and bowed head earned forgiveness for Bobby. He ended up on the stool in the corner. Seated as a spectacle and yet utterly alone, he muttered, "I'm getting out of here."

After the long and slow minutes finally yielded to the recess bell, Bobby stood to leave his seat, but was prevented by Mrs. Bredin. "Sit for a second, okay?"

Bobby moaned and slumped back. "It was because of Noah and he didn't even get in trouble. Am I still in trouble?"

"I expect more from you. And hitting is against the rules. You voted on the punishment, so you can't complain now. You are a smart boy, Robert. Don't let this keep you from doing the things you really want to accomplish."

"Really?" he asked.

"Really," she answered.

"Great," Bobby proclaimed as he hopped off the stool. "I've got a lot of work to do to accomplish what I want. See you after recess."

Bobby crossed the green field and approached a lone boy ostracized as a result of a wet smelly pants incident. "Hi Morgan."

"Aren't you going to call me Stinky like everybody else?" Morgan responded.

"What are you talking about?" responded Bobby in an exaggerated fashion. "The only thing you are is an awesome tag player. You were pretty much running faster than a dog."

Morgan's eyes brightened. "What kind of dog?"

"Probably a firefighter dog, or maybe a... a... racing dog, or a dog like the one on the Noonoos that's really fast, or a cheetah."

"Probly a cheetah cause they're the fastest of the jungle you know."

Bobby solemnly placed a hand on Morgan's shoulder. "And you're the fastest of the playground."

Morgan's chest swelled. "Yeah. I know. I pretty much am better than everybody. Do you watch the Noonoos?"

"Why, do you?" asked Bobby.

Morgan punched the air as he shouted, "They're the best!" He lifted his foot towards Bobby's stomach, hopping and stumbling in an attempt to keep his balance. "Yeah, I'm wearing my new shoes. They make me run this much faster." He ran in a several small circles to demonstrate. "See... how... fast ... I am?"

"Wow, that was even faster than ... than ... than this," Bobby said as he swung his arm in front of him in a quick jerking movement.

"So you know my dad says I'm pretty much the coolest guy in town."

"I can see why."

"Yeah. I know. I've probly got the biggest muscles in the class too."

"Let's see."

Flexing his bicep, Morgan shook uncontrollably. "See."

"Yep. The biggest muscles for sure. Almost as big as mine."

"Yeah. Almost. So, do you want to play with me?"

"I sure would, friend."

Bobby did not reveal his plans to his new ally right away; he spent nearly the entire recess building up his ego, solidifying the bond. Near the end of the break, while walking from the end of the field where they played towards the school, Morgan's step now mirroring Bobby's, follower to the teacher, Bobby said, "Wouldn't it be cool if you could leave school whenever you wanted?"

"Yeah it would be awe*some*."

Bobby divulged his plan. "I'm gonna leave school 'cause No-Duh stinks and Mrs. Bredin's a meany pants. If you help me leave today, I'll maybe help you some other time if you want to leave school 'cause somebody's not nice to you and the teacher blames you for it."

"Huh?"

"Morgan, if you help me get out of school today, I'll be your best friend," Bobby said.

"Okay." Morgan responded.

"So, when it's time for me to leave. You need to be a distraction," replied Bobby.

"A traction?"

"Yeah, a *dis*traction."

"Oh."

"Don't you think it would be pretty funny if someone pushed the sand table over?"

"Yeah, that would be funny."

"If someone did that it sure would be distracting."

"Tracting. Yeah."

"The kid who did that would be the coolest kid in school I think."

"Yeah, me too."

"Let's go into class."

After recess they both sat at the orange station: the sand table. Within a few moments, Mrs.

Bredin would signal that it was time to change stations.

"It's time for me to escape," Bobby whispered.

"Sweet," Morgan replied, still making a path in the sand for his toy bulldozer.

"I'll need you to make a distraction," Bobby reminded Morgan.

"Traction. Okay," Morgan replied.

"Remember how I said the person who pushed the sand table over would be super cool?"

"Yeah."

"Remember how distracting that would be?"

"Yeah."

"Right. So when I start to sneak out of the classroom, you push the sand table over, okay?"

Morgan froze. Before he said a word, Mrs. Bredin sang out, "Okay everyone, time to tidy up your station. We'll be switching in thirty seconds."

"So you're going to push the sand box over for me. Right buddy? Best friend?"

"Umm. I don't know."

"If you do it, I'll tell everybody you're the coolest kid."

"Umm. *O*kay."

"I knew I could count on you."

"Time to switch stations," Mrs. Bredin called.

Bobby flopped to his stomach and serpentined his way between the chairs, the legs and the tables on route to his escape from the classroom. Within a body-length of the door he sprung to his feet, took a step and placed his hand on the door knob.

"Bobby! What are you doing?" shouted Mrs. Bredin.

"Isn't it home time?" the boy with the dust streak along the front of his shirt asked his teacher.

"No it is not! Will you please dust yourself off and come back here?"

Bobby looked down at his shirt and then at the floor. "Stupid dirty floor gave me away," he muttered, until he looked towards the orange station. No mess, no distraction. Morgan avoided his eye contact as though not seeing was the same as not being seen. He sat at the un-tipped sand table. "You're not my friend any more... Stinky."

"Robert Tanner. What has gotten into you today? First you hit Noah. Then you try and leave the classroom. Now you make fun of Morgan. Shame on you. Please go sit in the corner."

"No. You go to the corner. You are not my mom and I don't have to listen to you. You are a big... a big... bum bum head," With that Bobby levitated off the floor and floated towards the front door, which opened allowing him to escape unimpeded.

"Close that door. Stop him. He's going to float into the sky," a bodiless female voice cried.

"Pardon me?" a bodiless male voice responded.

"Bobby get back to school! How could you just leave like that? What are you doing to our family name?" cried Marie.

"What are you talking about?" asked Jim.

"A glue stick is not worth going to prison over. It's against the law to fly without a pilot's license."

"Bobby has a pilot's license?" asked Jim in surprise. He had been quietly watching a television show; Marie was sleeping with her head on his lap.

"No he doesn't," affirmed Marie. "That's why he's going to jail. He should be in school right now."

Jim tentatively rubbed Marie's arm. "Bobby went to school today."

"But Bobby's not at school," she said, sitting up quickly.

"Of course he's not, he's upstairs in bed."

Marie swept Jim's hand away. "No, he flew out of the school. He was so rude. He's going to be grounded for a week."

"What do you mean he flew out of the school?" Jim asked.

"Hmm," Marie hummed as she lay back down. "Was I dreaming?"

Jim placed his hand back on Marie's arm. "Yep."

"Oh, sorry, I have the weirdest dreams when I'm pregnant." With that, Marie closed her eyes and slept.

ABOUT THE AUTHOR

MIKE JACKSON lives in Airdrie, Alberta Canada with his wife, Natasha and their five kids. Mike is the author of the Tanner Kids series, *Taven's Departing*, *Food for the King 2.0* and *The Adventures of My Grandpa Bert*.

www.mdjackson.com/author

Made in the USA
Charleston, SC
23 August 2014